D1356109

...should be re... ...ore the
last date ...

Usborne
Stories from India

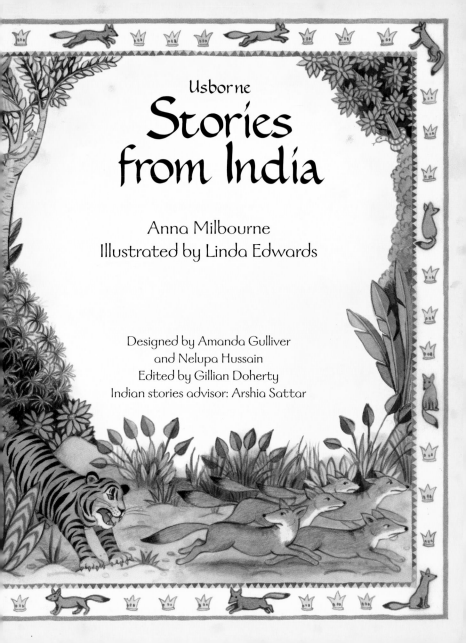

Usborne
Stories
from India

Anna Milbourne
Illustrated by Linda Edwards

Designed by Amanda Gulliver
and Nelupa Hussain
Edited by Gillian Doherty
Indian stories advisor: Arshia Sattar

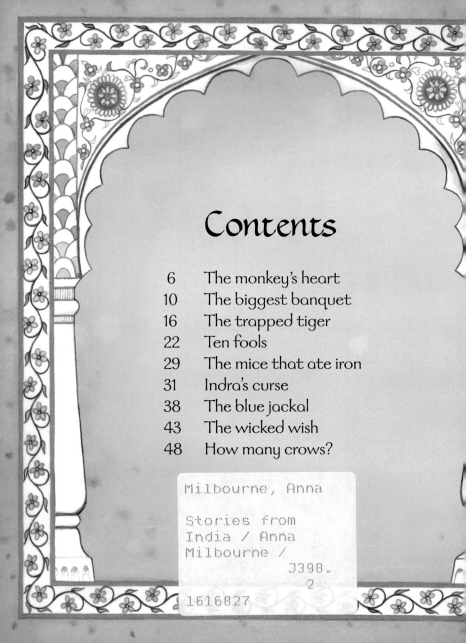

Contents

The monkey's heart

"All we ever eat is fish, fish and more fish," complained the crocodile's wife. "Wouldn't it be nice to have a change?"

"I've never really thought about it," the crocodile yawned as he basked in the hot sun.

"There's a little monkey that lives on the riverbank," said his wife. "It eats nothing but mangoes all day long. I bet its heart tastes deliciously sweet. Go and catch it – we'll eat it for dinner."

"It's too hot to be rushing around catching monkeys," the crocodile murmured.

"Too hot?" snapped his wife. "You mean you can't be bothered! Don't you even love me enough to feed me one tiny monkey's heart?" she sniffed, and two big crocodile tears rolled slowly down her face.

"All right. I'll see what I can do," sighed the crocodile, and he slipped into the river. He floated in the cool water, trying to think of a plan to catch the monkey. He wasn't the brightest of creatures, so it took him all afternoon.

As the sun was beginning to set, the crocodile swam over to the far riverbank, where the monkey was sitting in a mango tree.

"Hello up there!" he called to the monkey.

"Hello!" the monkey called back.

The crocodile smiled his largest, most inviting smile. "My wife and I," he said, "were thinking how nice it would be to have you for dinner – er, I mean – to have you *over* for dinner. We see you near the river so often and it would be good to get to know you better."

"That's very kind," said the monkey. "I'd love to come."

"We live on the other side," said the crocodile. "I can take you there on my back, if you like."

"Thank you very much," said the monkey, and he ran down the tree and hopped onto the crocodile's back.

When they were halfway across the river, the crocodile began to rock from side to side.

"Hey!" shouted the monkey, in alarm. "What are you doing?"

"Ha!" jeered the crocodile. "Did you really think I wanted to be your friend? It was a trick! Now my wife and I are going to eat your heart for dinner."

"Oh dear," said the monkey, shaking his head. "What a shame. You should have told me before we set off."

"What do you mean?" asked the crocodile.

"Didn't you know?" said the monkey. "Monkeys don't wear their hearts all the time. We only use them on special occasions. If you'd told me, I'd have brought it with me."

"Oh," said the crocodile, looking terribly disappointed. "I don't suppose we could go back and get it?"

"Of course," said the monkey. "It's hanging over there on that tree," and he pointed to a fig tree back on the riverbank.

The crocodile swam over to the tree, his mouth watering at the thought of the monkey's sweet heart.

As soon as they reached the bank, the monkey leaped off the crocodile's back and scampered up into the branches. Once he was safely out of reach, he stopped and looked back. "You fish-brain!" he laughed.

"Did you really think that monkeys keep their hearts in the treetops? So much for making friends with a crocodile. I'll never trust you again!"

So the crocodile and his wife never did get to taste a monkey's heart. For the rest of their days, they had to make do with fish – for breakfast, lunch and dinner.

The biggest banquet

Kubera was the richest person in the world. He was also a terrible show-off. He threw lavish parties and built huge temples and extravagant palaces, just so people could see how rich and generous he was. But no matter how much money he spent, he just seemed to get richer and richer.

One day, Kubera decided to hold the biggest banquet the world had ever seen. Anyone who was anyone would be there – the wisest scholars and the richest businessmen, the most important noblemen and the most powerful kings and queens. But that wasn't all. As his special guests, Kubera was going to invite the god Shiva and his wife, the goddess Parvati.

"Everybody's going to be so impressed," he thought, rubbing his chubby hands together. "I'm so fabulously wealthy that even the gods come to my palace to eat their fill."

Before long, all of Kubera's servants were bustling around his palace preparing for the great feast. They wrote invitations on perfumed paper and sent them all over the world; they bought jewel-encrusted goblets, gold and silver serving dishes, silken cushions and richly embroidered rugs; and then they began to prepare thousands upon thousands of dishes of mouth-watering food.

Meanwhile, Kubera went to visit the god Shiva. "Lord Shiva," he said, bowing down, "I am holding the biggest, most

10

spectacular banquet the world has ever known, and I would like you and Parvati to be my special guests."

Knowing what a show-off Kubera was, Shiva answered with a smile. "I'm sorry, Kubera, but we can't come. We have too much to do here."

"But you can't say no!" blurted Kubera. "I've already told everyone that you're coming."

Shiva raised his eyebrows. It was a risky thing to tell a god what he could and could not do.

After thinking for a moment, Shiva said, "My Ganesha enjoys a good banquet. He could come instead." Ganesha was Shiva's son – a short, fat boy with an elephant's head. He was a cheeky little god who absolutely adored his food.

"Thank you," said Kubera gratefully, and he hurried home.

The day of the banquet came and the palace hall looked magnificent. Servants scattered rose petals across the polished marble floors as Kubera waited eagerly for his guests.

When Ganesha arrived, Kubera led him to a special golden throne. "I'm hungry," said the little elephant god as soon as he sat down. Kubera clicked his fingers and servants appeared at once, carrying hundreds of dishes, all piled high with the most exquisite food imaginable.

Ganesha began to eat immediately. He gobbled up dish after dish of food without stopping. And in just a few minutes, every single dish in front of him was empty.

"I'm still hungry," Ganesha grumbled.

Kubera's servants rushed to bring him more food.

Ganesha ate faster and faster, so that soon he was licking dishes clean almost before they were laid down. In no time at all, he had devoured the entire banquet.

Kubera looked worried. He waved his hands at the servants, who ran off to cook more food.

"I'm hungry," wailed Ganesha. He stormed into the kitchen and started to eat the food that was still cooking. When that was all gone, he broke down the doors to the storerooms and gulped down everything he could find there. He ate and ate and ate. Soon, there wasn't a scrap of food left anywhere in Kubera's palace.

"I'm still hungry!" Ganesha trumpeted. He stomped back into the banquet hall and began eating the gold and silver dishes, chewing them up as if they were sweets. Then, to Kubera's horror, Ganesha picked up the throne he'd been sitting on and swallowed it whole. Next, he burst into Kubera's treasury and ate up all of his money and precious jewels.

"I want more!" Ganesha shouted, waving his fists and stamping his feet. But by now there really was nothing left for him to eat.

"If there isn't anything else," Ganesha said, "I might just have to eat..." – he swung around to look at Kubera – "YOU!"

Kubera turned and fled, and the little elephant god chased after him. They ran through the palace and into the gardens, across the city and over the hills.

"Come back," panted Ganesha. "I'm hungry!"

Kubera ran and ran until his legs felt like lead. Suddenly, stumbling breathlessly around a corner, he tripped and fell. He found himself at the feet of Lord Shiva.

"What's all this?" asked Shiva.

Before Kubera could reply, Ganesha ran up to them. "He doesn't have anything else for me to eat," he wailed, "but I'm still hungry!"

"Go and ask your mother for something," said Shiva, and, to Kubera's relief, Ganesha turned and headed for home.

Shiva helped Kubera to his feet. "So how did your banquet go?" he asked gently. "Was it impressive?"

Kubera was ashamed. "Not really," he mumbled.

"But I thought you were so wealthy and generous that even the gods eat their fill at your palace," chuckled Shiva.

Kubera blushed bright red. "I'm sorry for being such a show-off," he said quietly. Then his mouth dropped open in terror as he spotted Ganesha coming back. Without another word to Shiva, Kubera sped off down the hillside.

Ganesha giggled. "You don't have to run away any more," he called. "I'm full now!"

15

The trapped tiger

A man was walking through the woods one afternoon, when he came across a tiger trapped in a cage. "Excuse me," called the tiger. "Would you be so kind as to let me out?"

The man took one look at the tiger's rippling muscles and dagger-like claws and said, "Do you think I'm some kind of fool? If I let you out, you'll just eat me up."

"Come on now – I wouldn't eat you," coaxed the tiger. "If you set me free, I'll be in your debt forever."

The man looked doubtful.

"Oh please," sobbed the tiger. "I'm begging you." At the sight of a full-grown tiger crying like a baby, the man gave in. "All right, all right," he said. "I'll let you out. But remember what you said about not eating me."

He opened the door of the cage and out sprang the tiger. "Thank you very much," it snarled, and a slow, dangerous smile spread across its face. "Now I'm going to have you for my lunch."

"But — but that's not fair," stammered the man. "You just said that you wouldn't eat me."

The tiger threw back its head and laughed. "Fair?" it growled. "Who said anything about fair?"

It narrowed its amber eyes and stared at the man. Then it said, "I'll tell you what. In return for letting me out of the cage, I'll let you choose three judges. You can ask them whether it's fair for me to eat you. If they say it's unfair, I'll leave you alone. But if they think it's fair enough, you'll have to let me eat you up."

"Very well," agreed the man nervously. He looked around for somebody to ask, but there was no one in sight. So he walked up to the nearest tree and cleared his throat. "A tiger was trapped and I set it free. Is it fair if it eats me?" he asked.

The tree rustled its leaves. "Fair?" it whispered. "Is it fair that I offer men cool shade from the sun and, in return, they rip off my branches to feed to their cattle? Your fate is as fair as mine. What will be will be."

The man gulped as the tiger sharpened its claws. He hurried on through the woods. After a little way, he came across a buffalo turning a wheel at a well. "A tiger was trapped and I set it free. Is it fair if it eats me?" he asked.

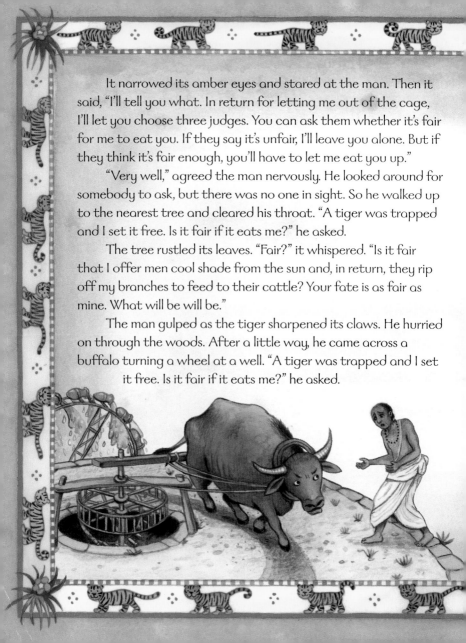

"Ha!" snorted the buffalo. "Is it fair that all my life I've given people my milk to drink and now that I'm old they make me walk round and round all day in the hot sun? Your fate is as fair as mine. Face it like a man!"

The tiger's belly rumbled loudly. In desperation, the man fell to his knees and asked the road. "A tiger was trapped and I set it free. Is it fair if it eats me?"

"Fair?" rasped the road, its voice a little dusty from lack of use. "Do you think it's fair that I show men the right way to go and just get trampled all over in return for my trouble? Your fate is as fair as mine. There's no way around it."

The tiger licked its lips in glee. "I think that just about settles it," it said. "Lie down here and prepare to be eaten."

Just then, a jackal came trotting by, whistling cheerfully. When it saw the tiger and the man, it stopped. "Hello," it said. "What's going on here?"

The man took a deep breath and told the jackal the whole story. When he'd finished, the jackal scratched its head. "How terribly confusing," it said. "Would you mind explaining it again?"

So the man explained all over again, while the tiger prowled around him, its tail twitching impatiently.

But the jackal still seemed confused.

"You mean to say that you were in the cage and the tiger came along – No, that's not quite right," it babbled. "You were in the tiger and the cage came along – No. What was it again? The cage was in the tiger—"

"Fool!" snapped the tiger. "I was in the cage and this man came along and let me out."

"I see," beamed the jackal. "I was in the cage – oh, but I wasn't anywhere near it. Oh dear, oh dear. You'd better go ahead with your lunch. I don't think I'm ever going to understand."

"Oh yes you are," snarled the tiger, infuriated by the jackal's stupidity. "Listen carefully. I'm the tiger, right?"

"Right," nodded the jackal.

"And I was in this cage, right?"

"Right," agreed the jackal. "Well, no, actually," it said, shaking its head and frowning.

"What's the matter now?" roared the tiger, almost bursting with rage.

"Well, if you don't mind me asking," said the jackal, "how did you get into the cage in the first place?"

"Through the door, of course," growled the tiger.

"How do you mean?" asked the jackal.

By this point, the tiger had completely lost its patience. It leaped into the cage. "Like this!" it roared. "NOW do you understand?"

"Oh yes, perfectly," grinned the jackal, and slammed the cage door shut. "And I think perhaps it's best if we leave it at that!"

Ten fools

"As emperor, I only ever meet wise and educated men," complained Akbar to Birbal, his trusted advisor. "I'm tired of meeting clever men, Birbal. I want you to show me ten of the biggest fools in my kingdom. I'll give you a month to find them."

"Oh I'm sure I won't need a month, sir," replied Birbal, and he set off at once. An emperor's orders, no matter how silly, must be obeyed.

Right outside the palace gates, Birbal met a man riding on a horse and trying to balance a huge bundle of firewood on top of his head.

"Why don't you put the firewood behind you on the saddle?" Birbal asked.

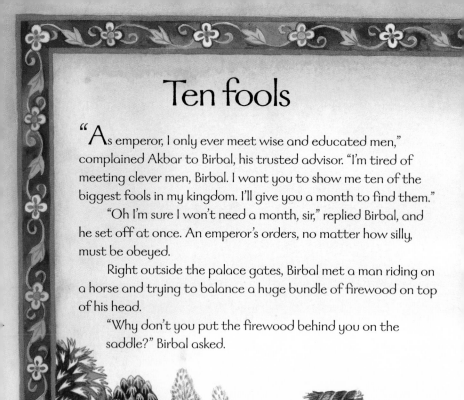

"The weight of the firewood as well as my own would be too much for my poor horse," said the man. "So I'm carrying the firewood myself."

Birbal nodded. "Come with me," he said, with a twinkle in his eye. "The emperor wants to meet you."

A little further along the road, Birbal saw a man lying in a ditch with his arms in the air. "Help!" shouted the man.

Birbal went to help him up. "Not my arms! Don't touch my arms," screeched the man.

"Why ever not?" asked Birbal, hauling him up by the waist.

"My wife has sent me out to buy a pot," the man explained. "She wants one this size — no bigger and no smaller. I was just on my way to buy one when I fell into the ditch. I couldn't get up without moving my arms. But if I move them, I'll never remember what size pot I'm supposed to buy."

"I see," said Birbal, swallowing a smile. "You'd better come with me. The emperor wants to meet you."

Birbal and the two men walked on. Before long, they saw a man running as fast as his legs would carry him. He tore right up to them and bumped into Birbal. "Sorry!" he gasped.

"What's the hurry?" asked Birbal.

"I was trying to find out how far the sound of my voice carries," panted the man. "So I shouted as loudly as I could and then I chased after it."

"Perhaps you could try again another day," suggested Birbal. "Why don't you come with me? I think the emperor wants to meet you."

They walked on until they came to a park. There, they found two men in the middle of a fierce argument. "What are you fighting about?" Birbal asked.

"We were both praying," explained the first man, "and I prayed that I would be given a buffalo."

"Right," nodded Birbal. It sounded sensible enough so far.

"And then my so-called friend here," continued the first man, "started praying for a tiger."

"It's a strange thing to pray for, I admit," said Birbal. "But why were you fighting?"

"Isn't it obvious?" shouted the first man. "His tiger is going to eat my buffalo."

"Yes," grinned the second man. "It is."

"You have to make it stop!" yelled the first, lunging furiously at his friend.

"Why should I?" crowed the second man. "It's hungry!"

Birbal shook his head in disbelief. "Will you stop fighting for a while and come with me?" he said. "I think the emperor wants to meet both of you."

Just then, another man walked up to them, with a pot of oil balanced carefully on his head. "You must be crazy to take them seriously," he said. "They've been fighting about it since the crack of dawn. No word of a lie! If I'm telling a lie, may my blood be spilled like the oil in this pot." And, to show what he meant, the man threw the oil he'd been carrying all over the ground.

"Oh no!" he cried forlornly, as his precious oil sank into the dust.

"Oh dear. Bad luck," said Birbal. "Come with me. The emperor wants to meet you too."

By this time, the sun was setting and Birbal started walking back to the palace, with the fools following behind. As they approached the palace grounds, they came across a man searching frantically on the ground.

"Have you lost something?" asked Birbal, bending down to help him look.

"Yes. I lost a ring over there," said the man, pointing to some bushes on the other side of the road.

"Why aren't you looking for it over there, then?" asked Birbal, looking baffled.

"Because the light's better over here," replied the man.

"Perhaps tomorrow will bring you better luck," Birbal smiled. "Why don't you come with me? I think the emperor will want to meet you."

In front of the palace gates, another man was digging hole after hole in the sand.

"Did you bury something here?" Birbal asked him.

"Yes — some gold pieces," said the man. "They're here somewhere, but I can't find them."

"Didn't you mark the place where you buried them?" asked Birbal.

"I didn't need to," said the man. "There was a nice fluffy cloud right overhead, marking the spot. But it seems to have gone now."

"Well, who would have thought it?" said Birbal, looking sympathetic. "You'd better come and meet the emperor," he said, and he led all eight men through the palace gates.

That evening, the entire court gathered to see whether Birbal had succeeded in his task. Birbal introduced his eight fools, telling their stories one by one.

The emperor laughed until he cried. "They shall each have a bag of gold for coming to see me," he said, wiping the tears from his eyes. "But, Birbal," he continued, "there are only eight fools here. I asked you to find ten."

"There are ten fools here, sir," replied Birbal.

"Then where are the other two?" demanded the emperor, looking around the courtroom.

"One is sitting on the emperor's throne and one is standing right in front of it," said Birbal, with a bow.

Everyone in the courtroom gasped as Akbar's face turned to thunder. Nobody called him a fool and got away with it. "Explain yourself," he said, glowering.

"If you'll forgive me, sir," said Birbal, "you and I are the biggest fools of all. You for setting such a ridiculous task and me for carrying it out."

There was a dangerous silence. But suddenly, to everyone's relief, the emperor burst out laughing. "Very good, Birbal," he said. "You too shall have a bag of gold for your pains. But as far as I'm concerned, you're priceless!"

28

The mice that ate iron

One morning, a young merchant was getting ready to go away on a long trip. Before setting off, he took his most valuable possession, a set of iron weighing scales, to a shopkeeper who lived nearby.

"I'm going away," he said to the shopkeeper. "My scales are too heavy to take with me, but I don't want anything to happen to them while I'm gone. Please could you look after them?"

"Of course," said the man. So the merchant left the scales there and went away on his trip.

When he returned, the merchant went straight to the shopkeeper's house and asked for the scales back. To his surprise, the shopkeeper shook his head. "I'm sorry," he said. "I'm afraid the mice have eaten them."

"Eaten them? But they were made of iron!" cried the merchant in disbelief.

"Well, the mice around here like the taste of iron," said the shopkeeper. "Especially good quality iron like that."

The merchant walked home deep in thought. "Who ever heard of mice eating iron?" he asked himself. "He can't be telling the truth. I bet he just wanted to keep my scales. But how can I prove it?"

29

The next day, the merchant went swimming in the river with the shopkeeper's son. They were good friends and often went swimming together. But this time, the merchant swam for just a little while and then said, "I can't stay for as long as usual. There's something I have to do." He left his friend splashing about happily in the river and started to walk home.

As soon as he was out of sight, the merchant began to run. He ran as fast as he possibly could, all the way to the shopkeeper's house. When he got there, he hammered on the door. "Something terrible has happened!" he shouted. "We were swimming in the river and an enormous bird came and carried off your son."

"What?" cried the shopkeeper, running out of his house and peering up at the sky. Then he frowned at the merchant. "But – but that can't be true," he said. "Birds can't just carry people off like that. It's impossible."

The merchant shrugged. "In a land where mice are strong enough to eat iron," he said, "surely a bird would have no problem carrying off a young man?"

The shopkeeper hung his head in shame. Without another word, he went into his house and brought out the scales. The merchant took them home, chuckling to himself all the way. And from that day on, the shopkeeper never, ever told him another lie.

Indra's curse

Once there was a man called Thintha. He had a wife called Kalavati, who everybody said was the most beautiful woman on earth. But, as Thintha knew, Kalavati was no ordinary woman; she was an apsaras, a magical being whose job it was to sing for the god Indra.

Every day, Kalavati flew up to heaven, and every evening, she came home to her husband. They lived very happily like this for a long time.

One morning, Kalavati said, "I'll be coming home late this evening. Indra has invited some of the other gods to a special celebration. He's asked all the apsarases to sing."

Thintha was suddenly seized with curiosity. "Take me with you," he begged. "I'd love to see what heaven is like."

Kalavati shook her head. "It's forbidden for humans to go there. If Indra found out..." She shuddered at the very thought.

"Just this once," coaxed Thintha. "I won't tell a soul." He pleaded and pleaded with her until, eventually, Kalavati agreed to take him. Using her magic, she shrank Thintha to the size of a caterpillar and hid him inside a lotus flower. Then she tucked the flower in her hair and went to Indra's celebration.

From his hiding place, Thintha
saw a world no human being had ever
even dreamed of. He watched gods float on
soft clouds; he listened to enchanted music; and
he heard the magical song of the apsarases, their
voices more delicate than a hundred crystal bells. Indra
even had a jester who, near the end of the evening, turned
himself into a goat and did a comical dance. It was the funniest
thing Thintha had ever seen. He laughed helplessly, clamping his
hands over his mouth so that
no one would hear him.

When the party was over, Kalavati took
Thintha home and turned him back to his normal size,
heaving a huge sigh of relief that they hadn't been caught.

The couple went back to their normal lives. The next day,
Kalavati went to heaven as usual and Thintha stayed behind.
His head was spinning with everything he'd seen, so he decided
to go for a walk. He wandered around the
market square, his mind full of gods
and clouds and music.

Thintha was picking his way through the market stalls, when suddenly he saw a goat that looked exactly like the one he'd seen the night before.

He rushed up to the goat and shouted, "Dance!"

"Goats don't dance," scoffed a passer-by.

"This one does," insisted Thintha. "Go on," he said to the goat. "I know you can. I saw you dance for Indra in heaven last night."

But the goat only stared at him with its yellow eyes.

"Go home and rest," laughed the goatherd. "The sun must have fried your brain."

Word spread around the city, and soon everyone was laughing about the madman asking the goat to dance. Before long, Indra got to hear of it. The god realized what must have happened and was absolutely furious.

He summoned Kalavati to him. "How dare you bring a human being into heaven," he thundered.

Kalavati trembled with fear.

"Say goodbye to your husband," Indra raged. "At midnight, you will be turned to stone. You will stand as a marble pillar in the temple. Only when the temple is knocked down will you be released."

Kalavati fled, sobbing, to Thintha and told him about the curse. Thintha hugged her and tried to comfort her. He knew there was nothing else he could do. Eventually, they both fell into an exhausted sleep.

When Thintha woke up the next morning, Kalavati was gone. He ran to the temple. There, in place of one of the pillars, was his beloved Kalavati, turned to stone.

"I'm so sorry," wept Thintha. "It's all my fault. But I'll find a way to set you free. I promise."

He sat by the pillar all day, racking his brains. The king would never agree to knock down the temple without a good reason. But nobody was ever going to believe that Thintha's wife had been turned to stone.

He thought long and hard. Just as the light of the setting sun began to spill through the temple door, an idea came to him.

He raced home, found four little pots and filled them with Kalavati's necklaces, bangles and other jewels. When night came, and the whole city was sleeping soundly, he crept into the deserted streets and buried them around the city.

Early the next morning, the first few people to emerge saw Thintha, disguised as a holy man, wandering about muttering. Word spread that a holy man had come to the city. The more Thintha wandered and muttered, the more people thought that he must be very holy indeed.

The king soon got to hear about the holy man and came to the market square to meet him.

Just as the king approached, a crow happened to fly overhead, cawing loudly. Thintha looked up and laughed. "Thank you, my friend," he called.

"You know how to speak to animals!" exclaimed the king. "Tell me. What did it say?"

"It told me that there is treasure buried beneath my feet," said Thintha. "You may have it, if you like. I've no need of it."

The king pointed at the ground. "Dig," he ordered one of his servants.

The servant dug a hole and uncovered one of the pots of jewels. He handed the pot to the amazed king.

The king and Thintha strolled about the city together talking. Soon, they found themselves in the middle of a park, where Thintha stopped. A moment later, a jackal called in the distance. Thintha smiled. "Thank you," he called back.

"What did it say?" the king asked eagerly.

"There is treasure buried underneath my feet," said Thintha. The king's servant dug again, and again he found a pot of jewels.

They walked on together a little further. To the king's astonishment, they uncovered another pot of jewels near the palace and a fourth right in front of the temple.

The king turned to Thintha. "I've never met anyone with such incredible powers," he said. "Come into the temple and let's pray together."

Inside the temple, Thintha stopped by the pillar where poor Kalavati was trapped in stone. Tears filled her stone eyes and began to run down her cheeks.

"What's this?" asked the king, astounded.

Thintha, whose eyes had also filled with tears, turned to the king and said, "She's weeping because you are going to die very soon."

"Die?" gasped the king. "Me?"

"Yes," nodded Thintha gravely. "You will die in three days' time if this temple is still standing."

"Guards!" shouted the king. "Knock this temple down. I want it gone by tomorrow."

That very evening, the temple was brought tumbling to the ground. Thintha watched anxiously and, as the last pillars fell, he saw a figure, just visible through the dust.

"Kalavati?" he whispered. The figure came closer. It was she. They fell into each others' arms, laughing for joy.

When Indra heard how Thintha had rescued Kalavati, he roared with laughter. He showered blessings on the happy couple and made sure they were never parted again.

The blue jackal

"Being a jackal is boring," thought the jackal as he roamed around the edges of the town one night. "I wish I was different."

The jackal was so deep in thought that he wasn't looking where he was going. He was just passing the cloth-dyer's house, when he slipped and fell into a deep tub. He leaped and scrambled, but try as he might, he couldn't climb out of the slippery tub. He had to spend all night sitting in the cold dye.

When the cloth-dyer arrived the next morning, he didn't look at all pleased to find a jackal in his tub of dye. Tutting crossly, he fished the dripping animal out and chased him away.

The jackal began to head home through the forest, feeling rather sorry for himself. He hadn't gone far when he met an elephant. As soon as the elephant saw him, it stopped in its tracks and stared.

"What are you staring at?" said the jackal. Then he looked down at himself and saw, to his horror, that the dye had turned him bright blue from nose to tail.

"What kind of a creature are you?" whispered the elephant.

"A blue one," groaned the jackal. He hung his head and waited for the elephant to burst out laughing. But the elephant

didn't laugh. Instead, it bowed down before him and continued on its way.

Further into the forest, he met a tiger. To the jackal's amazement, the tiger bowed down to him too.

"Perhaps it's not so bad being blue after all," thought the jackal as he trotted along. "I'm certainly different!"

When he arrived home, he caused quite a stir with the other jackals. "What on earth happened to you?" they asked, crowding around him.

The jackal smiled smugly. He had always longed for this kind of attention. "I can really make something of myself now," he thought.

He sat down, puffing out his chest importantly. "Last night," he said, "the forest goddess came to me. She crowned me king of the forest and turned me blue to mark my royalty. From now on, all the animals in this forest must do as I command."

The jackals looked at one another. None of them had ever heard of a forest goddess. But then, none of them had ever seen a blue jackal either. So they accepted him as their king.

Word quickly spread around the forest. Soon, all kinds of animals came to pay their respects to the new king. Monkeys fanned him with leaves, elephants served him his dinner and tigers guarded his camp. None of the animals realized that he was just a jackal.

With all of this attention, the blue jackal soon became so full of himself that he started to look down on the other jackals.

"I don't need to bother with the likes of you now," he boasted. "I have elephants and tigers to serve me instead."

He waved them away with his paw. "Be gone from my kingdom," he said. The jackals couldn't believe their ears.

"Go away or I'll set my tigers on you," snapped the blue jackal, and the tigers growled menacingly. Hurriedly, the jackals left the forest. They stopped in a field, fuming with anger at the way the blue jackal had treated them.

The oldest jackal spoke up. "I've got an idea," he said. "The other animals serve the blue jackal because they don't realize he's just a jackal, like us. But I know how we can make him show what he's really like."

As evening fell and the moon rose high in the sky, the jackals gathered together at the edge of the forest. "Now!" cried the oldest one, and they lifted their noses to the sky and howled.

The blue jackal hadn't howled once since he'd started pretending to be king – it wasn't a very fitting way for a king to behave. But now, as he heard his brothers' howls echoing across the treetops, he just couldn't help himself. He threw back his head and howled and howled with all his might.

The tigers, elephants and all his other loyal subjects stared at him suspiciously.

"He howls just like a jackal," said a tiger in disgust.

"Now you come to mention it," said an elephant, "he looks pretty much like a jackal too."

All the animals turned to the blue jackal and looked at him much more closely than they had before.

"We've been duped!" cried the tiger indignantly. "All this time we've been treating a plain old jackal like a king!"

And so, roaring, screeching, chattering and trumpeting in fury, the animals chased the blue jackal right out of the forest. And he never dared show his face there again.

The wicked wish

Bhasmasura was very, very wicked. He wished for nothing more than to make everyone – even the gods – afraid of him.

One day, Bhasmasura heard a story about a holy man who had prayed for so long that the god Shiva had appeared to him and granted him a wish. Bhasmasura thought this might be a good way to have his own wish granted, and so he sat down on the top of a mountain and began to pray to Shiva. He prayed non-stop for years and years. He sat there for so long that moss grew on his shoulders and birds began to nest in his hair.

Shiva was so impressed with Bhasmasura's dedication that he came to visit him. "You have done well to pray for so long," he said. "What can I do for you?"

"Nothing, my Lord," said Bhasmasura, with a cunning glint in his eye. "Just your blessing is enough for me."

This answer impressed Shiva even more. "There must be something I could give you," the god said. "Wish for anything you like and it shall be granted."

"Did you say *anything*?" Bhasmasura said, grinning wickedly. "In that case, I wish that anybody whose head I touch with my right hand will be transformed into a heap of ashes."

Shiva looked worried. This wasn't the kind of wish a good person would make, but he had said that he would grant Bhasmasura anything and so he had to keep his word. "Granted," he said reluctantly.

"Allow me to test out my new power before you go," Bhasmasura said, laughing nastily. And he leaped forward with his hand outstretched, reaching for Shiva's head.

Shiva ducked out of the way just in time.

With Bhasmasura close behind him, the mighty god fled. He raced over hills and tore through valleys, leaped over streams and scrambled through forests.

"How am I going to get out of this?" thought Shiva, as he stumbled towards a steep mountain.

"You look like you could use some help," said an amused voice. Perched on a rock high above Shiva's head sat the god Vishnu.

"Am I glad to see you!" Shiva gasped, trying to catch his breath.

"Hide here for a moment," said Vishnu. "Let me see what I can do."

Seconds later, when Bhasmasura came charging up the mountain, he found a woman standing in his path.

"Which way did Shiva go?" he demanded roughly. But he came to an abrupt stop when he saw the woman's face – she was utterly enchanting.

"Why don't you rest here for a while?" said the woman gently. "You look tired."

Bhasmasura was bewitched. "What is your name?" he asked. "I must have you as my wife."

The woman laughed, a soft, musical laugh. "My name is Mohini," she said, "but I cannot be your wife."

"Why not?" growled Bhasmasura.

"I can't marry anyone who doesn't dance as well as I do," said Mohini.

"I can dance just as well as you," leered Bhasmasura. "I'll show you. Any dance you do, I can copy."

Mohini glanced at his huge, hulking body and a smile appeared on her lips. "All right then," she said. "Can you do this?" She stepped away from Bhasmasura and danced a few steps, light as a feather on her feet.

Bhasmasura watched and then danced the same steps, his big feet scuffing up the dust.

Mohini nodded. "But can you do this?" she said, and twirled away from him. Round and round she danced, as gracefully as a swallow on a breeze.

Bhasmasura copied, flinging himself around like an overweight buffalo.

"Not bad," said Mohini. "But watch this. If you can copy me this time, then I'll marry you." And she danced on, moving so quickly this time that her feet were a blur. Then, turning to Bhasmasura, she placed her fingertips delicately on the top of her head and sank slowly down to the ground.

"Yes, yes," grunted Bhasmasura impatiently. "I can do that." The ground shook beneath his thumping feet as he leaped and twirled with all his might. Then, turning towards Mohini, he placed his right hand on top of his head and grinned. "You're mine, all m—"

But before he could finish his sentence, he had turned himself into a heap of ashes.

As Shiva stepped out from his hiding place behind a boulder, Mohini gave one last tinkling laugh and vanished. In her place appeared Vishnu, still smiling.

Shiva heaved an enormous sigh of relief. "Thank you, Vishnu," he said.

"Any time," Vishnu replied. And with that, the two gods set off together down the mountain, leaving the ashes to scatter gently in the wind.

How many crows?

Birbal was the cleverest of Emperor Akbar's nine advisors. There seemed to be nothing he didn't know. And so, from time to time, Akbar would amuse himself by putting Birbal's wisdom to the test.

One evening, the emperor was walking with Birbal in the palace gardens. It had been a hot day, and a number of crows were splashing about in the fountains. "I have a question for you, Birbal," said Akbar, twirling his moustache mischievously.

"At your service, sir," answered Birbal with a bow.

"How many crows live in my kingdom?" asked the emperor. He smiled to himself – surely even Birbal wouldn't be able to answer this question.

Without pausing to think even for a moment, Birbal replied, "Seven thousand, four hundred and thirty-eight."

"Come now, Birbal," said the emperor. "What if I have somebody count them and find out there are more than that?"

"Well, sir," said Birbal solemnly, "I can't account for crows from other kingdoms coming to visit."

"And if there are fewer?" asked Akbar.

"I can't account for crows going away on trips either, sir," said Birbal, without even the hint of a smile.

"Honestly, Birbal," said Akbar, laughing, "you really do have an answer for everything!"

The great battle

Once there were five brothers. The eldest, Yudhistira, was a just and noble leader; the second, Bhima, was stronger than any other man on earth; Arjuna, the third, was a master archer; and Nakula and Sahadeva, the youngest, were brave and loyal twins. Their uncle was king and had one hundred sons of his own. As children, the five lived with their many cousins. The king employed the best teachers for them, and they grew up to be skilled warriors.

When all the boys were old enough, the king divided his kingdom between them. To his own sons, he gave the best part; and to the five brothers, he gave a small patch of desert that no one else wanted.

But the five brothers were happy with their share. With Yudhistira leading them, they worked hard and built cities and luxurious palaces. Soon, their small patch of desert had become a wealthy and beautiful kingdom.

Duryodhana, one of the king's sons, grew jealous of his cousins. "They'll want our kingdom next," he said to his ninety-nine brothers. "We must find a way to get rid of them."

After brooding for a number of days, Duryodhana came up with a plan. Yudhistira had always been terrible at dice games, but he was never able to resist them. "This," thought Duryodhana craftily, "will be my cousin's downfall."

So he challenged Yudhistira to a game, in which each round would be played for money. His cousin eagerly agreed to play.

On the day of the game, Yudhistira and his brothers arrived at Duryodhana's palace. The king, his court and hundreds of other people gathered in the grand hall to watch.

As Yudhistira sat down, Duryodhana said casually, "By the way, I won't actually be throwing the dice myself – Uncle Sakuni is going to throw for me."

At this, a low murmur rippled around the hall, and the five brothers exchanged worried glances. Sakuni had never been known to lose a dice game. Nobody knew whether or not he cheated, but whenever Sakuni played, he won.

The game began and, sure enough, Sakuni threw well every time. At first, the bets were small – a handful of pearls, a sack of gold. But soon, Yudhistira, caught up in the excitement of the game, began to place larger and larger bets.

He bet beautiful palaces and precious temples, and lost. He bet acres of land and grand cities, and lost again. But he kept on playing — over and over again — until his entire kingdom and everything in it belonged to Duryodhana.

"My dear cousin," sneered Duryodhana, "what can we play for now? You have nothing left."

At this point, the king interrupted. "Enough is enough," he said. "This could start a war if we're not careful. Let your cousin keep everything he's lost."

Duryodhana scowled at Yudhistira. But he couldn't very well disobey the king. "All right," he said. "Keep it."

But as his cousins were getting ready to leave, Duryodhana hissed in the king's ear, "Father, that isn't going to solve anything. Our cousins have been made to look weak in front of all these people. If we don't act quickly, they'll start a war anyway, to get their revenge."

The king looked anxious. "What can we do?" he said.

"Leave it to me," said Duryodhana, with a sly smile. He turned to face Yudhistira. "I challenge you to play one more game," he said. "If you win, then you can leave here with your head held high. But if I win, you and your brothers will be banished. You'll have to live in the forest, out of my sight, for thirteen long years. Dare you play again?"

The hall fell silent as everybody waited for the reply.

"Let's play," said Yudhistira.

And so they played again. But the outcome was no better.

"I win!" Duryodhana laughed. "Well? What are you doing still standing here?" he spat. "Get out!" And he threw his unhappy cousins out of the palace.

For thirteen long years, the five brothers kept their word. They hid in the forest, living a poor and simple life.

As the thirteen years drew to a close, Duryodhana became nervous. "When our cousins return," he said to his brothers, "they'll be angry and want revenge. We must fight and kill them."

The five brothers had friends in many different kingdoms, and so they soon found out about their cousin's wicked plan. While Duryodhana gathered an army against them, they set about gathering their own. The two sides grew larger and larger, as warriors came from every corner of the earth to join them.

In the midst of all this, Arjuna went to visit Krishna, a friend and distant cousin, to ask for his support. But Duryodhana arrived at the same time, wanting Krishna's help too.

"You're related to both of us," said Duryodhana. "So you can't help one and not the other."

"Very well," Krishna answered thoughtfully. "To one side, I will give my army of a million men. To the other, I will give myself alone. But I won't fight during the battle. I'll only offer advice."

He gave Arjuna, the youngest of the two, first choice. Without hesitation, Arjuna said, "I choose you, Krishna. A good friend is worth a thousand armies."

"You numbskull!" Duryodhana scoffed, and went away delighted with his million men.

The idea of going to war with their cousins made the five brothers miserable. "Let's ask them one more time if we can solve this without fighting," Yudhistira suggested. So they asked Krishna to visit Duryodhana as their messenger.

"Your cousins don't want to fight you," he told Duryodhana. "They've sent me here to ask for peace."

Duryodhana just laughed in his face.

"Very well," said Krishna. "In seven days' time there will be a new moon. Let the battle start then."

Seven days later, the two armies came face to face. Looking across the battlefield at all the people he knew, Arjuna felt too sad to fight. "It's no good," he sighed. "I can't fight them. It's not right."

Krishna looked at him quietly. Then something very strange happened. Before Arjuna's eyes, Krishna began to grow. He grew and grew until his body filled all the space between the earth and the sky, and stretched from horizon to horizon. It was a truly terrifying sight.

"I am the god Vishnu," he thundered. "I was born into a man's body in order to battle wickedness. Your cousins have brought this war upon themselves. You must fight them now so that justice may be done."

"I understand," Arjuna cried out.

At once, the figure began to shrink. It got smaller and smaller until it fit into the chariot, and Arjuna was left staring speechlessly into the eyes of his good friend Krishna.

A conch shell was blown, breaking the silence, and the battle began. With a deafening roar, the two sides charged at each other. Bhima rushed forward, wielding his mace; Arjuna could barely be seen behind his whirlwind of arrows; the twins fought back to back in a blur of swords; and Yudhistira directed the rest of the army, shouting orders from an elephant's back.

Horses galloped and chariots raced, elephants trampled and men fought with all their might. Thunder rumbled and the earth shook. It was the biggest battle there had ever been.

All the time they were fighting, Duryodhana complained to his men. "You're not trying hard enough!" he yelled. "Don't just stand there. Kill them!" His bitterness spread, and soon all of his men were bickering. Unable to work together, his army fell apart.

Duryodhana fled to save his own skin.

Enraged by his cousin's cowardice, Bhima searched high and low for him, tossing elephants and chariots out of the way as though they were mere toys. At last, he found Duryodhana cowering among the reeds of a lake.

Duryodhana looked terrified. "I won't fight you, Bhima. You're beneath me!" he said, trying to muster a sneer.

"This is for starting this senseless battle!" roared Bhima, bringing his mace down on his arrogant cousin.

With Duryodhana crushed and deserted, the battle was finally over. Exhausted but victorious, the five brothers returned to their kingdom to cheers and celebrations. And for many years afterwards, Yudhistira ruled the kingdom wisely and well.

A bull from heaven

A monk was on his way to the temple one morning, when he noticed some enormous hoofprints beside the water tank.

"I've never seen an animal with feet that big," he thought, scratching his bald head. "I wonder what it could be." He tried following the prints to see where they went, but after a few paces they stopped, as if the creature had vanished into thin air.

The following day, he found more hoofprints on the other side of the water tank.

"I have to find out what this creature is," thought the monk determinedly. So the next morning, he got up really early and ran all the way to the water tank. He hid himself in the bushes, and waited for the mysterious animal to appear.

He hadn't been waiting long when a huge, dark shadow fell over him. The monk looked up, and his eyes nearly popped out of his head with astonishment. A gigantic bull with a shining golden coat was flying down from the sky. It landed next to the water tank, dipped its nose in the water and drank thirstily.

After a few minutes, the huge creature snorted, pawed the ground and took a giant leap back into the air. Its rope-like tail swung over the bushes where the monk was hiding, and, without thinking, he reached out and grabbed it. The next thing he knew, he was being swept up into the air.

Up and up they flew. The monk clung on for dear life as the water tank, the temple and all of the countryside dropped away beneath him.

The wind whistled past his ears as the bull sailed higher and higher. They flew so high that soon there was nothing to see but empty sky all around. Terrified, the monk closed his eyes.

Just as he was beginning to wonder how much longer he could hold on, the monk felt himself land on something soft. He opened his eyes cautiously, one at a time, and saw the most glorious sight.

Soft, fluffy clouds lay beneath his feet, and all around him were golden dishes of big, sticky sweets and sugary cakes, and goblets filled with fragrant drinks.

The monk couldn't believe his luck. He picked up a plate of sweets and tried one. It was scrumptious! Then he took a sip from one of the goblets. His tastebuds tingled with delight. There was nobody in sight, so the monk sat down and helped himself. He drank and ate, and ate and drank, until he was fit to burst, and then he lay down and fell asleep.

When he woke up, he discovered that all the plates he'd eaten from were full again, as were the goblets. So he sat down happily to eat and drink some more.

The monk stayed in this strange place for several days without seeing anyone at all apart from the bull. At first, he was happy just eating and sleeping. But after a while, he grew lonely.

Early every morning, the bull flew away, but it always came back a few hours later. "It must fly down to the water tank," thought the monk. "That means I can go home, visit my friends, and then catch a ride back again whenever I like."

So the next time the bull began to snort and stamp its feet, ready to take off, he crept up behind it and gently took hold of its tail. The huge animal leaped into the air, with the monk clinging tightly behind.

Down they flew, through the clouds and into the open sky. The monk could see the water tank far below them. It grew closer and closer as they plummeted through the air. Before long, the bull landed, and the monk tumbled to the ground behind it. He picked himself up and ran to the temple to see his friends.

"Where have you been?" asked the other monks, crowding around him. "How come you've grown so chubby?" The monk told them all about his adventure. When they heard about the delicious sweets, their mouths watered and their bellies rumbled. "Take us back there with you," they pleaded.

The monk agreed. "With my friends there to keep me company, I'll never have to leave again," he thought happily.

The next morning, the monks all crowded into the bushes by the water tank. As the bull flew down to land, they jostled for a glimpse, elbowing one another and giggling with excitement.

As the bull took off, the first monk grabbed hold of its tail and was swept into the air. The second monk grabbed hold of the first monk's feet and sailed up behind him. The third took hold of the second monk's feet. The fourth took hold of his, and so on, until all of the monks were swinging in a long chain behind the bull.

Up and up they soared, the wind whistling past their ears. Far too excited to be afraid, the monks started chatting about the amazing sweets they were about to eat.

The monk at the very bottom of the chain shouted up to the top, "Tell us again how big the sweets are."

"About this big," shouted the monk at the top, cupping his hands. But, of course, as he did so, he let go of the bull's tail.

"Help!" the monks screamed as they fell. Down and down they tumbled, one after the other.

SPLASH went the first monk as he landed in the water tank. Then SPLASH, SPLASH, SPLASH — the others fell on top. Bruised and dripping, they heaved themselves out of the water.

Meanwhile, the bull went on flying up into the sky, getting higher and higher until it disappeared from view.

The next day, the monks waited eagerly for the bull's return, so they could try their luck again. There was no sign of it all day.

"Perhaps it will come tomorrow," they said to one another. But it didn't come then, or the next day either.

Day after day they waited, in the hope that the bull might come again. But it never did.

The emperor's moustache

One afternoon, Emperor Akbar strode into the courtroom where his nine advisors were waiting and said, "I have a very serious question for all of you. If somebody pulled the emperor's moustache, what do you think would be a suitable punishment?"

Eager to impress him, the emperor's advisors started to suggest various punishments.

"He should receive a hundred lashes," said one.

"No," said another. "He should be trampled by a herd of elephants."

"Burn off his toes!" volunteered a third.

The emperor shook his head. Then he turned to Birbal, who hadn't yet said a word. "And you, Birbal – what would you say?"

"He should be given sweets, sir," Birbal answered.

The other advisors looked shocked. Surely Birbal would be punished for such impudence.

"And why is that?" asked Akbar.

"Because the only person who would dare to pull your moustache, sir, is your little grandson," said Birbal. "It would seem harsh to treat him any other way."

A broad grin spread across Akbar's face. "You're quite right, Birbal," he said. "Well done."

Lord Moon

"Stop that! Watch where you're going!" cried the little hare as an enormous elephant trod on her tiny home, squashing it flat. But the elephant paid no attention.

Ever since they'd arrived at the lake, the elephants had been making the hares' lives a misery. It wasn't that the hares minded sharing the water — it had been a very dry summer and this was the only lake in the area that hadn't dried out. But as the elephants stomped around with their huge, clumsy feet, they squashed the hares' homes, frightened their children and

made their ears ache with all the endless trumpeting.

The hares had tried everything to make the elephants stop, but now, even the oldest, wisest hare had run out of ideas. "Elephants take about as much notice of us as they do of the ants. There's simply nothing we can do," he shrugged.

"Nothing we can do?" muttered the little hare furiously as she rebuilt her home for the fifth time that week. "I'll see about that!"

That very night, as she gazed at the moon's reflection shimmering on the surface of the lake, the little hare came up with a plan.

The next evening, the little hare marched over to the largest, clumsiest elephant, who seemed to be the leader of the herd, and cleared her throat importantly.

The elephant leader swung his great head around, first looking left and then looking right. He didn't notice the little hare standing right by his toes.

"Hey!" shouted the little hare, scrambling up onto a large rock. "I'm HERE!"

The elephant peered at her. "Oh!" he trumpeted in surprise. His voice was so loud, that it almost blew the hare right off the rock. "Who are you?"

"I am a messenger," the little hare said, sitting up very straight and trying to look official. "I have been sent by Lord Moon to speak with you."

"I'm listening," boomed the elephant.

So the hare continued. "This lake belongs to Lord Moon, and the hares who live here have been specially appointed by him to guard it. You've been giving us all kinds of trouble with your thoughtless ways and your clumsy feet, and Lord Moon is very, very angry."

"I didn't know the lake belonged to Lord Moon," said the elephant doubtfully. "In fact, I've never heard of him."

"You've never heard of Lord Moon?" The hare staggered backwards, looking shocked. "Well, you can see him in the lake, as plain as the trunk on your face. Take a look."

The elephant looked and, sure enough, there in the middle of the lake, shimmering majestically on the surface of the water, was the moon. The huge animal gasped in awe.

Bending close to the elephant's ear, the hare whispered, "Be careful. He's really angry. But if you bow down to him and apologize, he might forgive you."

"Bow?" said the elephant. He shook his head slowly. "Elephants don't bow."

"Oh," said the hare. "Well, don't mind me. I'm only a messenger. I only suggested it because Lord Moon is so angry, and when he gets angry..." She shrugged and turned away. "I just wouldn't like to see you get hurt, that's all."

69

"Wait!" cried the elephant, and he pointed at the lake with his trunk. "Look at Lord Moon. What's he doing?" A gentle breeze had started to blow, rippling the surface of the lake and making the moon's reflection tremble.

"He's shaking with rage," whispered the hare. "Bow! Bow quickly! Apologize before it's too late."

To the hare's delight, the elephant bowed down low to the moon's reflection. "Lord Moon," he said, "please accept my deepest apologies for the trouble we've caused."

Just then, the breeze blew a little harder, making the moon's reflection quiver even more. "Oh dear," said the hare. "Look! You've made him even more angry."

"Oh no," the elephant moaned fearfully. "What can I do? Please help me."

"Let me try," said the hare. She bowed down so low that her ears touched the ground in front of her. "Lord Moon, please forgive the elephants," she said. "They are truly sorry and they promise never to come here again."

The breeze dropped, leaving the moon's reflection still and calm on the surface of the lake.

The elephant heaved a huge sigh of relief. "Thank you. Thank you!" he said gratefully.

After bowing once more to the moon's reflection, the elephant gathered his herd and left. All the elephants crept away on tiptoe, so they wouldn't disturb Lord Moon's hares, who were just settling down to sleep.

70

A hundred questions

It was a scorching hot day, and five brothers had been walking for hours through the forest. Gasping with thirst, they threw themselves down under a tree to rest.

While the other four lay in the shade, Nakula, the second-youngest brother, shinned up the tree to see whether there was any water nearby. "There's something glittering between the trees way over there," he called to his brothers as he clambered back down. "Wait here a minute. I'll go and have a proper look."

He followed the path between the trees. Gradually, it became more and more overgrown, but Nakula kept on going, fighting his way through the knotted vines until, suddenly, he stumbled out into the open. There before him was the most beautiful lake he'd ever seen. Blue lotus flowers floated on its surface, and the water was so clear that he could see the pebbles on the bottom.

He knelt down and was about to drink from the lake when a voice boomed out of nowhere, "This lake is mine! Before you may drink my water, you must answer my questions."

Nakula looked all around, but there was no one to be seen. So he bent down again and took a sip. Immediately, he fell down dead.

After a while, Nakula's brothers began to wonder where

he was. "I'll go and look for him," said Sahadeva, his twin.

Sahadeva's throat was so dry when he reached the lake that he ran to the water without even noticing his dead brother.

Again, the mysterious voice boomed out its warning. Sahadeva glanced around, but didn't see anyone. Shrugging, he took a sip of water, and he too fell down dead.

Next came Arjuna. He was so relieved to find water that he didn't see his brothers lying dead on the ground.

"This is my lake!" cried the voice. "To drink here, you must first answer my questions."

Arjuna whipped out his bow and fired arrows in the direction of the voice. They shot right over the lake and clipped the trees on the far bank.

There was a moment's silence, and then a deep chuckle echoed across the lake. "You won't get around it that easily. Answer my questions and you may drink."

Arjuna hesitated – he was unbearably thirsty. "I'll just take a gulp of water first," he thought. But as soon as the water touched his lips, he dropped down dead.

Bhima, the strongest of the brothers, came next. He rushed to the lake without seeing his brothers' bodies, and dipped his huge hand into the water.

"Stop!" the voice rang out. "Drinking this water will kill you unless you answer my questions first."

"One little sip is hardly going to kill me," Bhima guffawed. A moment later the earth trembled as he crashed to the ground.

When Yudhistira, the eldest brother, came to the lake at last, he found all four of his beloved brothers lying dead beside the beautiful, sapphire-blue water.

"What has happened here?" he whispered in horror.

Sorrow for his lost brothers welled up inside Yudhistira and he began to sob. But his body was so parched with thirst that not a single tear fell. He waded, heartbroken, into the lake and bent to drink, so that he would have water for his tears.

"This is my lake," warned the voice. "Do not drink without my permission unless you want to end up like your brothers."

"I'm sorry," sighed Yudhistira, wading back to shore. "I didn't know the lake belonged to anyone. I won't take your water without permission. What must I do?"

"Answer my questions," boomed the voice.

"But who are you? Whom shall I answer?" asked Yudhistira.

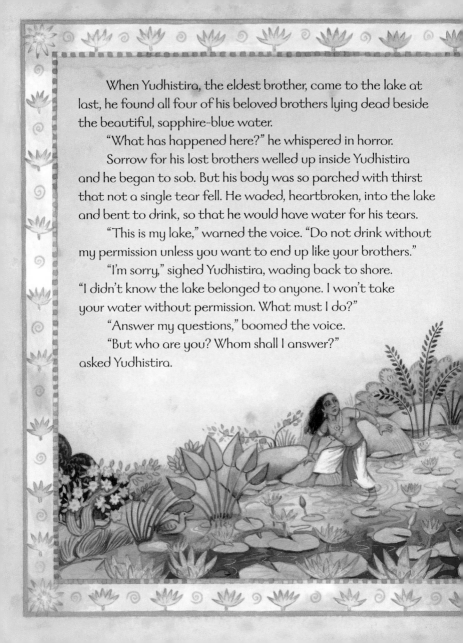

On the other side of the lake, a lone stork appeared. It picked its way across the bank, then shook its feathers and flew off over the trees.

Then all at once, the lake began to swirl and froth. A gigantic figure burst out of the water. It grew and grew until it towered above Yudhistira.

"I," it thundered, "am the god of the lake. It is I whom you must answer."

"Very well," gasped Yudhistira in amazement.

And the questions began.

"What is important for somebody who sows seeds?"

"Rain."

"What is faster than the wind?"

"The mind."

"What are more plentiful than blades of grass?"

"Our thoughts."

The questions came so quickly that Yudhistira barely had time to answer one before the next rang out. His throat raged with thirst, but, bravely, he carried on.

"What doesn't move after being born?"

"An egg."

"What is the greatest wealth a man can possess?"

"An education."

Yudhistira's voice cracked. But the questions kept on coming, thick and fast.

"What sleeps with its eyes open?"

"A fish."

"What is the friend of someone about to die?"

"The good they have done in their lifetime."

Finally, it was over. Yudhistira fell to his knees, clutching his burning throat. He had answered one hundred questions.

"You may drink," said the god.

Faint with thirst, Yudhistira put his parched lips to the cool, fragrant water. With the first gulp, he felt his body flood with life. Two more gulps and he felt more refreshed than ever before.

"You have answered my questions well," said the god. "So well, in fact, that you may choose one of your brothers to come back to life."

"Thank you," said Yudhistira. "If I may choose only one, then I choose Nakula."

"But Nakula is only your half-brother. You are very fond of Arjuna and Bhima. Don't you want them to live?" asked the god.

"Of course I do," said Yudhistira. "Nakula and Sahadeva were born to a different mother, it's true. But I love all my brothers equally. I'd like them all to live, but I may choose only one. And so I choose Nakula. This way, at least each mother will have one son left."

"That is a good and noble answer," said the god, nodding.

77

"In fact, you have answered so well that you can have all of your brothers back."

Yudhistira gave a cry of joy and rushed over to where his brothers lay. One by one, they slowly came back to life, rubbing their eyes and yawning as though they had merely been asleep.

"Go now in peace," said the god of the lake.

All five brothers watched in awe as the magnificent figure sank slowly back into the foaming lake. A moment later, there was no sign that the god had been there at all – apart from a trail of bubbles floating silently on the water.

The little birds and the mighty sea

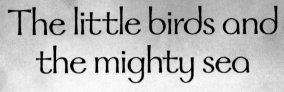

Down on the seashore, close to the lapping blue waves, stood two little birds. They were husband and wife, and they were looking for a place to build their nest.

"Here's a good spot," said the husband. "It's got everything we could possibly wish for – a beautiful view, a lullaby of waves to send our children to sleep..."

"Here?" spluttered his wife. "I can't lay my eggs here. When the tide comes in, it will wash them out to sea!"

"What kind of father do you think I am?" cried her husband indignantly. "I'd never let the sea take our eggs away." He puffed up his chest feathers and stared commandingly across the water.

"Don't be silly," said his wife. "A small bird is no match for the sea."

But her husband only smiled and preened his wing feathers. She tried coaxing, scolding, begging and pleading, but nothing seemed to work. Her husband simply would not listen to reason.

"Trust me," he said. "It will be absolutely fine. I'm not going to let the sea wash our eggs away."

"Fine!" said his wife. "Have it your way." So they dug a nest in the sand and she laid a clutch of four tiny eggs in it. Then she settled down on them and watched anxiously as the waves crept up the shore, slowly swallowing up the sand.

Her husband strutted back and forth in front of her, glaring at the sea. When the water was just a feather's breadth from the nest, he held up his wing and said, "Stop! That's quite far enough."

At that moment, a very large, foam-topped wave lurched up out of the sea and began rolling in to shore.

"Stop!" shouted the little bird. "I said stop!"

But the wave rolled on. It came closer and closer, growing all the time, until it towered right over him.

"Stop!" he squawked. But the wave didn't stop. It began to topple over. The little bird seized his wife and fluttered into the air just as the wave came crashing over their nest.

The couple watched in horror as their precious eggs were swept away.

"Our poor children!" wept the wife.

"Don't worry," said her husband helplessly. "I'll – I'll think of something."

But he couldn't think of anything a little bird could do to stop the mighty sea. So he went to visit Garuda, king of all the birds.

"Lord," he said, bowing down, "we did nothing to harm the sea, and yet it stole away our eggs. Please help us."

"I'll try," promised Garuda. "Go home and comfort your wife." So the little bird went back to the seashore. The couple waited, huddling forlornly on the wet sand.

But Garuda couldn't think of anything a bird king could do to stop the mighty sea. So he flew up into the air and cried out to the creator of the earth, sea and sky, "The little birds did nothing to harm the sea, and yet it stole away their eggs. Please help them."

Garuda listened for a reply, but heard nothing. He was about to turn back, thinking that his cries had been in vain, when something very strange happened. An enormous wave rose up out of the sea, and balanced on the very top were four tiny eggs.

The birds watched, open-beaked, as the wave came closer and closer. It had almost reached them when it began to curl over. Slowly but surely, the entire wave bent over until its tip was almost touching the sand. Very, very gently, it placed the eggs at the little birds' feet. Then, with an almighty crash, the wave collapsed, and the foaming water rushed back out to sea.

"There," croaked the husband, once he had managed to find his voice. "What did I tell you? It all turned out splendidly!"

But he helped his wife dig a new nest out of reach of the rolling waves – just to make absolutely sure.

Rama and Sita

Rama was a good and kind prince. So when his father announced that Rama would be the next king, everyone was delighted. Everyone, that is, apart from his stepmother. When she heard the news, she flew into a rage and stormed about the palace shouting.

The king rushed to her side. "What is it, my love?" he asked anxiously. "Are you ill? I'll do anything to make you feel better."

"Anything?" asked his wife slyly.

"I promise — anything," the king said.

"Then send Rama to live in the forest for fourteen years and make my son, Bharata, king instead," demanded his wife.

The king was horrified, but he had given his word, and a king, of all people, can't break his promise. So, with a heavy heart, he ordered Rama to leave the kingdom.

Rama went to break the news to his wife, Sita. "I'm coming with you," was her immediate reply.

"Me too," said Lakshmana, Rama's closest brother.

Word of Rama's banishment spread like a flood – everyone who heard the news broke down in tears. It was the saddest day the kingdom had ever known. Flowers wilted, songbirds fell silent and even the sun lost its warmth.

The forest where the three went to live was a dangerous place, with monstrous demons lurking in every shadow. As Rama, Sita and Lakshmana walked further and further into the gloom, demons followed, hiding behind the tangled trees.

Deep in the heart of the forest, the demons sprang out and attacked. Rama and Lakshmana stood on either side of Sita and defended her from the monsters' terrible teeth and slashing claws.

After a furious scuffle, the demons fled, howling. Nursing their cuts and bruises, not to mention their wounded pride, they went straight to their king for help.

The demon king was a horrible, ten-headed monster called Ravana. When he heard of Rama and Lakshmana's bravery, he was filled with rage. "How dare they!" he bellowed. Jumping into his magic chariot, he flew to the forest to kill them himself.

But when Ravana saw Sita, all ten of his jaws dropped open. She was the loveliest creature he had ever seen. He decided then and there to capture her and make her marry him.

A little while later, a golden deer came bounding through the trees. It stopped right beside Sita.

"What a pretty creature," Sita exclaimed. She went to stroke it, but it dashed away into the forest.

"I'll catch it for you," said Rama, running after it. Moments later, they heard Rama's voice, shouting, "Help! Lakshmana, help!"

"Rama's in trouble," cried Sita. "Hurry, Lakshmana! Go and help him."

So Lakshmana ran to find Rama, leaving Sita all alone.

Suddenly, Ravana leaped out from the bushes, his ten ugly mouths sneering. "Ha! My little trick worked," he laughed.

"What do you mean?" asked Sita, backing away.

"Help! Lakshmana, help!" Ravana mocked, in a perfect imitation of Rama's voice. Seizing poor Sita, he flew away with her in his magic chariot.

By the time Lakshmana and Rama realized they had been tricked, it was too late. Sita was gone. The brothers wandered for weeks in the forest, searching for her. Rama was heartbroken. He couldn't eat or sleep, he was so unhappy.

Then one day, as they were searching, they came across a monkey. But this was no ordinary monkey — it was as big as a man, and as they approached, it stood up and bowed.

Rama and Lakshmana had never seen anything like it before. But they bowed politely to the monkey in return.

The monkey peered into Rama's sad, pale face. "What is it that troubles you?" it asked in a gentle voice.

Rama stared in astonishment. But, seeing how kind the creature's eyes looked, and how wise its face, he told the monkey everything. After listening carefully, it said solemnly, "My name is Hanuman. Let me help you."

Rama and Lakshmana followed Hanuman to his troop of monkeys, who all agreed to help. The monkeys told more monkeys, and these monkeys told their friends the bears. Soon, all over India, thousands of monkeys and bears had joined the search for Sita.

After weeks of searching, Hanuman and his troop reached the seashore. They were staring forlornly out to sea, wondering where to look next, when an eagle flew over. "Are you looking for a woman?" it called. "The demon king took her. He lives on the island of Lanka, far out to sea."

The monkeys turned to Hanuman in despair. "How will we find her now?" they said. "We can't swim!"

Without answering, Hanuman turned and climbed the hill behind them. Then he began to run. The ground trembled as he thundered down to the water's edge. With an almighty leap, he soared high into the air. Fish gasped at the sight and sea monsters swam up from the deep just to watch. In a single bound, Hanuman crossed the sea and landed safely on the island of Lanka.

He hunted all over the island for Sita. At last, he found her imprisoned in a grove of trees, guarded by lots of ugly demons.

When night fell, Hanuman slipped past the demons and hid in a tree. "Rama has sent me to find you," he whispered to Sita. "Help is on the way."

"Please hurry," Sita whispered back. "If I don't agree to marry Ravana by the end of the month, he says he's going to tear me to pieces!"

"Take heart," said Hanuman. "We'll save you." And he raced back to tell Rama the news.

Rama, Hanuman, the monkeys and the bears marched to the seashore and built an enormous bridge stretching all the way across the sea. Then they charged across to Lanka, to fight for Sita's life.

Ravana's entire army was waiting for them. There were big demons and little demons, one-eyed demons and three-eyed demons, demons with hairy ears and pigs' faces, all screeching and screaming horribly.

As soon as Rama's feet touched the shore, he whipped out his sword and rushed fearlessly into battle. All around him, monkeys and bears hurled rocks and tree trunks at the oncoming monsters.

Then, just when Rama's army was starting to win, a demon sneaked up behind Lakshmana and shot him in the back with a poisoned arrow. Ashen-faced, Lakshmana staggered and fell.

The monkey doctor hurried to his side. But when he saw the wound, he shook his head. "If I had special herbs from the Himalayan mountains," he sighed, "I might be able to heal your brother. But as it is, he will die."

"No!" cried Rama.

Hanuman sprang into action. He bounded back over the bridge and all the way to the Himalayas, speeding faster than time itself. He picked up an entire mountain, heaved it onto his shoulders and carried it all the way back to Lanka.

The doctor plucked the herbs he needed and mixed them together. As soon as he fed them to Lakshmana, his wounds began to heal, and within an hour he was back on his feet.

More determined than ever, Rama slashed his way through the battling hordes until he reached Ravana. "Your beautiful wife is mine. All mine!" taunted the demon king.

Rama swung his sword and chopped off one of Ravana's heads. But the head grew back at once. Rama sliced off another. But that grew back too. Soon, he was chopping and slicing heads in a blur. But, each time, the heads just grew back, and the ten ugly mouths laughed and laughed.

Rama fell back, exhausted.

"Poor Rama," mocked Ravana. "Never to see Sita again."

Furious, Rama drew ten arrows. He set fire to them and shot with such speed that the demon didn't even see them coming. With a burning arrow in each of his ten foreheads, Ravana fell to the ground. The terrible demon was dead.

When they saw their king fall, all the other demons fled for their lives. Free at last, Sita ran joyfully into Rama's arms, and the monkeys and bears danced and hugged one another.

Longing to share the news of the victory with his family, Rama asked Hanuman if he would go and tell them.

"Of course," said Hanuman, and he sped off immediately. Within the hour, he was back again, hardly out of breath, and holding a message for Rama.

The message read: "Please come home. I never wanted to be king instead of you. I am just taking care of the kingdom until its rightful ruler returns. Your loving brother, Bharata."

So Rama, Sita and Lakshmana said farewell to their friends and left the forest. Hanuman bounded ahead to tell Bharata the good news. Even before they could see the gates of the city, they heard the cheers of jubilation welcoming them home.

The story of the stories

Many of the stories in this book are thousands of years old. They have been told time and time again, passing down from one generation to the next. Some, such as the tales of Akbar and Birbal, can be traced back to real people and events. However, each time a story is retold, it changes a little. After so many retellings, it's impossible to tell how much of a story is true, and how much has been woven from imagination. Most of these stories are so old that nobody knows who told them for the very first time. There are even stories about where the stories could have come from.
One such story goes like this:

On a summer's evening long, long ago, the god Shiva and his beautiful wife Parvati were sitting in their palace in heaven. "Tell me a story," said the goddess to her husband.

"Gladly, my love," Shiva answered.

"But not just any old story," pouted Parvati. "I want one especially for me. One that nobody in the universe has ever heard before."

So Shiva told Parvati a story.

It was a good one, and the goddess was utterly absorbed from beginning to end. "That was the best story I've ever heard!" she squealed in delight. "Tell me another."

94

The god laughed and told her another one, and then another, and another, until Parvati's eyes drooped with tiredness, and she fell fast asleep.

But the goddess wasn't the only one to hear the stories. One of Shiva's servants had come to see him. When he heard his master talking, he paused outside the room, not wanting to interrupt. He overheard the beginning of the first story and was completely enthralled. Unable to drag himself away, he listened to story after story, pressing his ear against the door so he wouldn't miss a single word.

When Shiva had finished, the servant ran home, bursting to share these wonderful tales. His wife adored the first story so much that she made him stay up all night to tell her the rest.

The servant's wife worked in the palace as Parvati's maid. As she was arranging the goddess's hair the next morning, her head was full of the fabulous stories she'd been told. To amuse her mistress, the maid began to tell them.

Parvati listened for a few minutes, then she got up and stormed out of the room. She was furious. Marching up to her husband, she shouted, "You promised to tell me stories that no one had ever heard before."

"Yes," said Shiva, looking confused. "And that's what I did."

"Even my maid knows those stories!" yelled Parvati.

Shiva called for the maid at once. "Who told you the stories?" he asked.

"My husband," said the maid timidly.

So Shiva summoned her husband. "Where did you get the stories from?" he demanded, his eyes flashing dangerously.

With his knees knocking together in fright, the servant confessed. "I listened at your door," he said. "I didn't mean to. I overheard the first little bit by accident, and then I just had to listen to the rest. I'm sorry for telling my wife too," he added. "But the stories were *so* good, I couldn't help myself."

"In that case," raged Parvati, "you can go and tell them to the whole world! And don't you dare come back until every single person on the planet knows them."

So the poor servant was banished from heaven. He wandered the earth, telling the stories he had heard to everyone he met.

For all anyone knows, he may be telling them still.

With thanks to Irving Finkel, for his advice
about the dice game in 'The great battle'.

This edition first published in 2005 by Usborne Publishing Ltd,
Usborne House, 83-85 Saffron Hill, London EC1N 8RT, England.
www.usborne.com Copyright © 2005, 2004 Usborne Publishing Ltd.

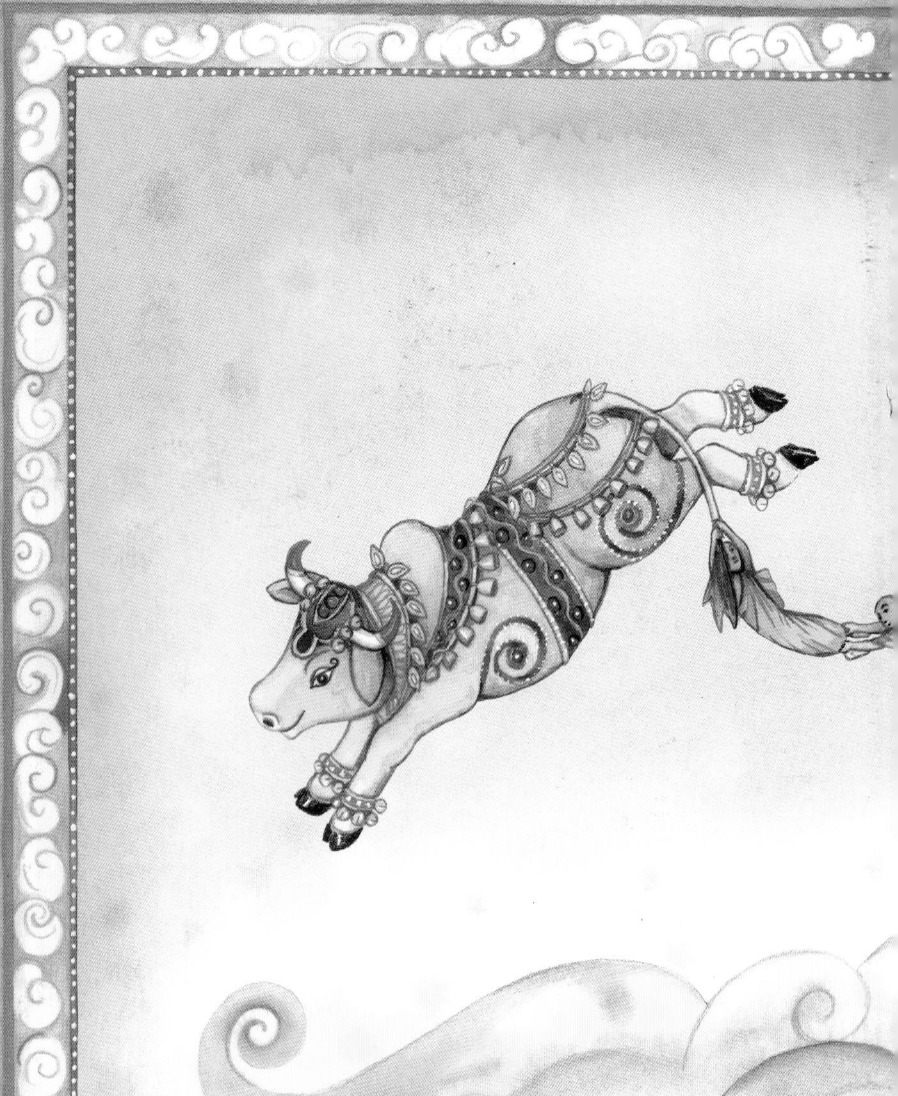